DE HISTORIA ET VERITATE
UNICORNIS

ON THE HISTORY AND TRUTH
OF THE UNICORN

Discovered and Annotated by Michael Green

Millis Public Library
Auburn Road
Millis, Mass. 02054

39936

NOV. 1 0 1989

RUNNING PRESS
BOOK PUBLISHERS
PHILADELPHIA ◇ PENNSYLVANIA

SO-AHI-525

JH
813.54

Library of Congress Cataloging in Publication Data

Green, Michael, 1943–
  Unicornis: on the history and truth of the unicorn.
  Summary: An illuminated manuscript setting forth the
fictional fifteenth-century diary of one Magnalucius, who
records his first-hand observations of unicorns along with the
facts he has learned about their natural history.
  1. Unicornis—Fiction. 2. Unicorns in art.
[1. Unicorns—Fiction. 2. Unicorns in art. 3. Latin language
materials—Bilingual] I. Title.
PS3557.R3753U5 1983   813'.54 [Fic]   83–3168
ISBN 0-89471-216-0 (deluxe ed.)
ISBN 0-89471-207-1 (lib. bdg.)
ISBN 0-89471-206-3 (pbk.)

Copyright © 1983 by Michael Green. All rights reserved under
the Pan-American and International Copyright Conventions.
Printed in Hong Kong by Leefung–Asco Printers Ltd.
Canadian representatives: General Publishing Co. Ltd., 30
Lesmill Road, Don Mills, Ontario M3B 2T6. International
representatives: Worldwide Media Services, Inc., 115 E. 23 St.,
N.Y., N.Y. 10010.

9   8   7   6   5   4
Digit on the right indicates the number of this printing.

This book may not be reproduced in whole or in part in any form or by any means
electronic or mechanical, including photocopying, recording or by any information
storage and retrieval system now known or hereafter invented without written
permission from the Publisher.

This book may be ordered from the publisher.
Please include $1.50 postage. But try your bookstore first.
Running Press Book Publishers, 125 South 22nd Street, Philadelphia, Pennsylvania 19103.

NFBF
4.98

Table of Contents

STAMP OF THE
ancient Brotherhood whose library
preserved the UNICORNIS manuscript
down through the centuries

THE DISCOVERY

In the fall of 1982 I received a letter, handwritten in an elegant italic script, requesting a meeting with me as soon as possible "on a matter of the greatest possible concern and mutual advantage." I was, the letter claimed, "perhaps the most qualified person" available for an unnamed undertaking. It bore a curious closing: "In amore unicornis," and was signed, "Frater Iamblicus."

Having passed through the esoteric sixties, I am no stranger to arcane personages with mysterious errands. This opportunity sounded too promising to pass up, and so I wrote back, inviting Frater Iamblicus to my studio.

Within the week, a thin, cowled figure was sitting before me, carefully holding a well-wrapped bundle. In grave, precise phrases and a hard-to-place accent, my visitor began by complimenting me on The Unicorn Notebook, which I had recently illustrated. To my puzzlement, he claimed that my drawings were "most faithful depictions" and asked if I had ever actually seen the animal. I replied—appropriately, I felt—"Not yet!" adding that my illustrations were strictly a work of imagination.

This answer seemed to satisfy him, and he studied me solemnly. "Would you like to see the Holy Beast?" he asked, folding back the paper from his package to reveal a time-worn leather portfolio. As he untied the intricate knots that secured its covers, he recited under his breath a short litany that must have been Latin. Then, almost with a flourish of pride, he laid the covers open before me.

Gazing at the voluminous contents, I felt a sense of awe and amazement. Page after yellowed page was filled with notes and jottings, accompanied by delicately-tinted drawings of unicorns and a few brilliant miniatures. They were executed in a curious mixture of Medieval and Renaissance styles, and from their tattered and discolored margins, it was clear that they were very old indeed.

"This," said Frater Iamblicus, "is the *Codex Unicornis*—The History and Truth of the Unicorn. *It is the testament of the venerable Master Magnalucius, and the treasure of our Collegium Gnosticum, which he founded. Originally, in the fifteenth century, our order was gathered on an estate near Ravenna. Now we are dispersed across many countries, but we are united by Magnalucius's teachings, the heart of which is the secret Doctrine of the Unicorn. . . ."*

No doubt this man was serious. Carefully I examined the handsome notes and sketches. They certainly appeared authentic, but still I felt bewildered. Were the unicorns depicted on these pages supposed to be allegorical, or literal? But my visitor's conspiratorial manner clearly assumed I was beyond that sort of question.

"For centuries," he went on, "our fraternity and its lore have been concealed. But now we must break our silence and spread these teachings without restraint."

"Why now?" I found myself asking. In

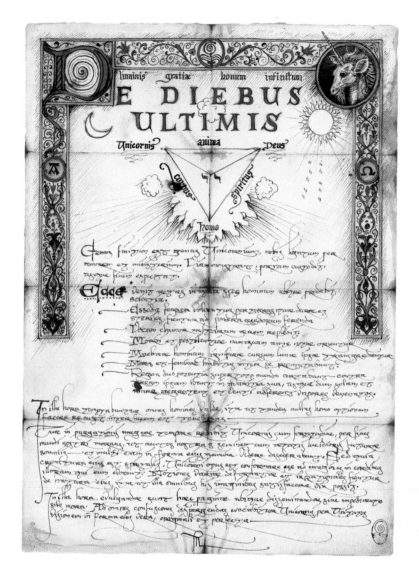

reply, Frater Iamblicus drew from the portfolio the yellowed sheet of vellum pictured here and translated it for me:

❧The Unicorn is a kindred race, bound to us in love and service. He points the way, he guards the gate, he waits until the end.

Behold! an age shall come when science shall darken everywhere the hopes of men. Chariots of iron shall roll the land, which shall grow hard and barren to bear their weight. The air shall be filled with a clamor of many voices. Un-

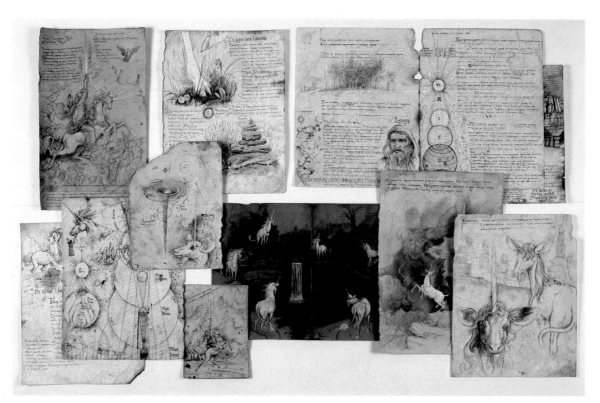

known plagues and sicknesses shall arise. The sphere of the Moon shall bear the booted heels of Man.

Two mighty kingdoms will contend for all the world, and turn against it, until the soil and the sea shall sicken and the wind become a flux of poisoned vapors. And all men shall be sorely tried, so that at the last, none may escape the choice between Light and Darkness.

Then, in the Time of Great Purification, will the Unicorn return in strength, lingering at the margins of our realm, to seed our minds with dreams of a brighter age to come; and many shall hunger to see him in his true shape. But being a spiritual creature, the Unicorn must conform himself to the images held in the hearts of those who call him forth. And there shall be so many ill-formed and conflicting ideas as to his nature, that he can hardly find a way to satisfy them all.

Then must these pages be revealed and broadcast without restraint; that all confusion may be resolved and a unity of vision call forth the Unicorn in his true, original, and perfect state. ✦

"This does seem to be the right time," I agreed. "But how can I help you?"

"One way to broadcast this manuscript would be to reproduce it in a book," Frater Iamblicus replied.

"But perhaps not all of it. . . ." I considered. "And the writing would have to be translated—"

"So it was prophesied!" he cried. "Select three sheets to show to your publisher, and to no one else. I will visit you again in one week's time."

When again Frater Iamblicus called, I had good news: Running Press had quickly recognized the manuscript's worth and was keen to publish a facsimile edition. And so, with my new friend's help, I set to work. One page at a time, the manuscript was translated with the help of a brilliant young classical scholar, and then photographed.

As the book neared completion, I received yet another visit from Frater Iamblicus. "My friend," he said gravely, "a decision that our brotherhood has long avoided now draws near. Will you visit our hermitage, that we may obtain your counsel?"

That weekend, I arrived at the mountain-top retreat of the Collegium Gnosticum, a community of perhaps a dozen robed anchorites — earnest and friendly, but a somewhat melancholy group. After a simple lunch, Frater Iamblicus led me to a tiny chapel in the woods nearby. We entered, bowing through the low door, and sat in silence for a time. At length he spoke, with obvious reluctance.

"Now you shall see the Horn!"

Opening a narrow wooden casket that sat on the low stone altar, he chanted "Nunc ex tenebris te educo [Now I bring thee out of darkness]" and lifted out a spiral horn. I must admit that a physical thrill passed through me at the sight of the strange object's wild beauty. It was mounted in a heavy, ornamental silver base set with purple stones and inscribed with runes which, I guessed, were Celtic in origin. Certainly it was the most magical and mysterious device I'd ever seen. It seemed charged with arcane secrets, and I could not take my eyes off of it.

"Touch," said Frater Iamblicus, "and know that the Unicorn is neither symbol nor allegory."

The Horn was cold, far harder than ivory — and very real.

"The Horn is even older than its setting," he continued, "and that is old enough. It has en-

7

dured through fire and floods, and felt the grasp of saints and kings. It is a talisman of sovereign power that can even draw the living Unicorn within its compass. But here is its doom: only by its rightful owner can its virtue be quickened. In any other's keeping, its light will dim and fade. So," he sighed, addressing the treasure in his hands, "we have given away our secrets, and now we must release thee, too, and consign thee to an unknown fate. For you see—" He fixed his sad eyes directly on my own. "—its powers sleep, even in the hour of greatest need."

"You mean your brotherhood is not the rightful owner?" I asked.

"No. For generations, we have passed the Horn down from master to disciple. In our pride, we came to think we had risen above the Rule."

De historia et veritate Unicornis

"What rule is that?"

"That no man knows to whom the Horn should go. That ever and again it must be hidden so that, in obscurity, it may draw its rightful owner to its side. Thus it is said—'In silver bound, beneath the ground, awaits the spiral Horn.' The faith that it shall be found again—a faith we have not had—renews the precious link between the Unicorn and Mankind."

I was amazed at his frank confession. "So now you must hide this Horn?"

He nodded. "And perhaps you have a part to play. Please listen to the final prophecy of Magnalucius." From the box he lifted a short scroll. "Again, I shall translate. . . ."

The work was a poem of sorts that began:

Into darkness will I fade
Into a night that Man has made,
But through that gloom shall gleam the Sun
When I am lost, and again am won.

Then its meaning became obscure; the only line I understood immediately had to do with the "new lands across the sea."

"Well?" asked Frater Iamblicus, asking me to pronounce the inevitable.

"I suppose the scroll describes the sort of place where the Horn should be buried."

"Yes, yes! But where?"

For the next three days, we pored over the words of the scroll and combed through the pages of Magnalucius's Codex for further clues. Finally, as I was strolling in a meadow to clear my thoughts, the perfect place came to mind. And like most riddles, it now seems simple in hindsight.

Frater Iamblicus agreed that my solution fulfilled the scroll's intent, and insisted that we set out for the chosen spot that very afternoon. We went alone and laid the Horn into the earth within a box of brass, marking the spot in such a way that one versed in the lore of unicorns would recognize it.

"Now it is gone," said Frater Iamblicus, "and a new age is dawning that will sweep us all aside." But as we walked away, he frowned: "Suppose the Horn is never discovered?"

I had wondered the same thing myself. "Perhaps we should reproduce the scroll at the end of the book." To this, Frater Iamblicus agreed.

Now all this has been accomplished. The book is ready to be published, so that anyone can study these strange and wonderful pages. But

I know that many readers will still have doubts. Is the manuscript really authentic? Does the Unicorn really exist?

There are no further proofs, and that, I believe, is as it should be. The Unicorn is a creature of mystery and of faith, not a specimen to be caged or dissected. Indeed, when these pages have crumbled into dust, it is the mystery that will endure, and not the explanation.

Michael Jonathan Green
East Fallowfield, Pennsylvania
1983

FROM MAGNALUCIUS'S JOURNAL

Monday in March, Being the Vernal Equinox

Planting begun in earnest, but I must record a singular event. Shortly after daybreak, as is my habit, I walked in contemplation through the alder groves bordering our river. There I glimpsed a forest creature altogether white in color—a hart, I now believe, but cannot be certain, for it was moving through thickest brush all greening with new leaves. Now this was the remarkable thing: I was balanced in a most inward state of devotion, yet this curious creature did not draw my attention outward, as is the irksome habit of intriguing objects. Instead, I stood awhile in a most pleasurable stillness of mind and spirit; for the beast seemed as much within me as without, among the alders. But when my curiosity quickened enough to speculate on what species of creature I beheld, it vanished forthwith.

May the loving God protect us and our Master.

[from a previous page]

. . .no longer do we wonder by what means such pure souls, set quite loose from the world, find their way to our remote society. Those who belong, arrive. So be it!

Friday, of March the 26th

Again I have glimpsed the white beast, and I marvel at God's works, for I strongly suspect it is the fabled Unicorn!

Having finished tilling the westernmost field and leaning on my spade, I fell to gazing on a great vine of honeysuckle in new bloom upon the ruined wall. Upon me, unbidden, came a speechless joy at that Divine Hand that guides to perfection every stem and leaf and petal; and I was lifted up and saw the flowery mass as never before, glowing with a celestial and jewel-like light.

How long I gazed thus, I know not, but at length I grew mindful that in the center of this extraordinary sight was the head of an animal, regarding me with great kindly eyes that showed no fear. On his forehead was set a single horn, white as ice. The sight of this singular device sent a thrill up my back. I believe I swooned, for the next I knew I was sitting on the earth, and the creature was no more to be seen.

I know it will not be wise to speak of this hastily.

The Saturday Following

Donkey-wagon broken; an iron axle-shaft to be obtained. The blessed Eugnostos remains in retreat.

Sunday, of March the 28th

This morning, Sylvanius baked wonderful breads—a triumph since our store of flour is so low. All afternoon I vainly searched the fields and wood for any sign of the white beast with one horn.

Monday, the Next Day

In the forenoon broke a tremendous thunderstorm. Fortunately most of the planting was finished. I found a most curious pebble, possibly of glass, by the waterfall. It appears to be a natural . . .
[the page breaks off]

The First Sunday after Easter

About the second hour of the morning, Sylvanius, our excellent cook, was seated at the edge of the forest that overlooks our garden. Not far away, I was gathering herbs and greenery for the cure of fever. Now Sylvanius was deep in contemplation, as is his custom, when there approached him a white creature. There could be no mistake—its single horn was white and shining: it was a unicorn. In full view it stood, only a few paces from Sylvanius, regarding him as silently as the fall of dew.

Whether the cook saw the animal or not, I could not tell, for Sylvanius made no outward sign or motion. For near an hour the two remained thus, Man and Unicorn, neither moving at all. Nor did I budge from where I watched, awestruck.

There was a slight odor of spice, like cinnamon. I do now believe that Sylvanius and the creature were conversing, one with the other, in the brightness of their minds.

I do not dare to speak to anyone of this mystery. Rather, I shall await the return of our Master, who can untangle this for me, for he is a man learned in all the knowledge that men possess, and more besides.

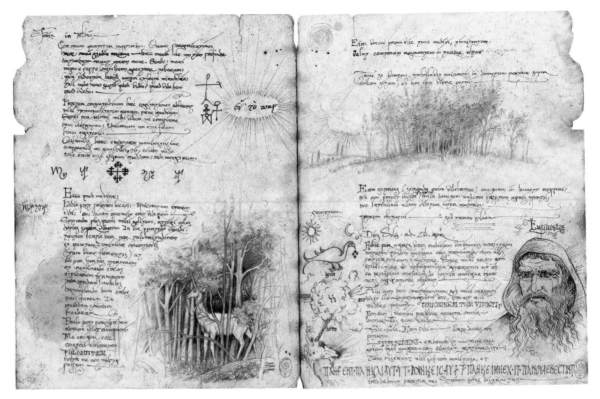

The Wednesday Following

The mystery of this beast has seized my heart! All my wanderings and secret studies have not stirred me so deeply. I feel as if I stood on the deck of a noble ship and gazed upon a foreign land in which are seen strange adventures and wondrous deeds.

Yet this is no ordinary obsession, for my thoughts bring me a rare tranquility, almost a joy. I seem to catch sight of this truth: the Unicorn is not the true center of this mystery. For although this creature is most manifestly sensible and corporeal, yet at the same time I know he is a kind of sign, a portent.

Such are my thoughts; for today, a little after first light, I saw the creature again, and I shall tell how. Wandering farther afoot than usual, I came to the twin hills overlooking the vineyard. In that abundant meadow, I was so taken by the quiet and beauty of the Lord's creation (all in the flush of springtime), that I threw myself down upon the grass and then, lying back like a child, looked up at the sky. Gazing at the clouds that sailed overhead, I fell into a reverie.

Some time after, I sensed a fragrance, as of cinnamon. And sitting upright, lo! I saw the favored beast, all shining and not many paces away. And for this first time I heard his voice, solemn yet musical, like a distant bell echoing in a tall tower.

Then turning himself, the unicorn walked into the small grove of trees that crowns the slope, and I could see him no longer. I followed after (for it seemed that I should), but nowhere in the copse did I find him. But neither could the animal have fled unseen, for those trees are everywhere surrounded by open meadow; nor is there any hiding place among them.

Of this matter I am amazed. Yet shall I continue my silence.

Sunday, of April the 11th

As I labored in the fields this day I heard voices calling that our Master had at last finished his long retreat. I ran to greet him, hoping to beg for his private counsel on the matter of this perplexing beast that so dominates my thoughts.

Others were already with him, but as I hurried up, he turned to me, saying loudly that all might hear, "And hast thou seen the Unicorn?"

I had forgotten that from him, no secrets are concealed. So great was my consternation that all I could reply was simply, "Yes."

"At last!" he cried. "And dost thou think that thou alone hast seen the creature?"

Then all the others laughed, but not with ill intent, and left me standing in confusion.

---

132 grossi
 62 grossi—earned by the carpentry of Taddeo
194

Wednesday, of April the 14th

Our Master came upon me by the ruined fountain and bade me speak.

"What is this Unicorn," I asked, "that he may disappear?"

"The beast cannot disappear," Eugnostos replied. "He merely leaves our realm and passes to another."

I asked, "What other realm is there?"

"Hast thou no knowledge of the Four Ages?" he inquired of me.

(Which knowledge I did have from the writings of Plato; the first being the fabled Golden Age, then the Ages of Silver and of Bronze, and now, lastly, a final Age of Iron.)

And our Master asked me: "Are these Four Ages not akin to the great dynasties that chart the failing history of mankind?"

"They are," I replied.

"And yet they are not!" he said. "Or rather, more than that."

Then he led me into the garden and seated me on the Bench of Learning, and covered my head with his own cloth, and instructed me. I am confounded, for he gave me a great teaching in whose light all things are seen anew.

"Attend well," he said. "Each of these previous ages continues still, *for they were not measures of the changing years upon this world we know, but rather are other realms where Man has sojourned before arriving here.*

"The first is called the Age of Gold, because it is as radiant with golden light as a thought newborn from the mind of God. Each age that follows is a further elaboration of that theme; there being three more steps by which divine thought is finally congealed into our Age's dense and inert matter. Altogether, the realms are as the four notes of a powerful chord that spans all that was, or is, or ever shall be.

"Man has occupied each realm and, each time failing in his oath and promise, was removed to a lower, coarser one. The others are invisible to us—yet every age endures, intermingling with the rest, the warp of one serving as the other's woof."

As Eugnostos spoke, a great stillness had come over the garden. Standing quietly by the trees was the Unicorn: his eyes wide and bright, his ears attentive as my Master continued his account:

"Know thou," he said to me, "that the Unicorn is a creature of the Golden Age, which is his proper home. But as the enduring friend of Man, often he joins us in our exile, for he can cross the threshold of the ages. And when he departs from us, he does not disappear, but simply passes through a portal."

Then I asked: "May we pass through these portals also?"

"Indeed!" the blessed Eugnostos replied. "No man can regain the paradise from whence he came, except that he journey back across those realms. Yea, many have passed therein. Their gates are never far, though the realms are artfully concealed, the finer within the coarser, and each entrance is a riddle difficult to discover without the proper guide. For some, the Unicorn serves as guide. And he has chosen thee!"

fact, she seems acquainted with the creature's very thoughts and feelings.

Tomorrow I journey to Firenze with Piero the Elder.

To be purchased:
sound drawing papers from Rizzoletti
manuscript vellum, 2nd quality
inks, glycerine, gum arabic
steel pens
ground colors: blue, green, brown
needles
a knife, suited to kitchen use
peppercorns

[Continued from a previous page, not shown:]

. . . different from the several schools and collegia wherein I have studied.

Sylvanius goes into retreat at first light tomorrow, and I am selected as tomorrow's cook. Lord have mercy on us all, for my vast and catholic knowledge, garnered from so many lands and peoples, does not include practical use of the oven.

Says Eugnostos: "All knowledge is vain, except where there be work; and all work is empty, except where there be love."

Tuesday, of April the 20th

My first day in the kitchen. We are now 21 mouths to feed. To my aid came an angel in the form of Johannes' daughter Isabella; and for that, I believe the others are thanking God.

Again I am humbled. Never had I concerned myself overmuch with Isabella, for she is but 16 years of age. But this day I found her a delightful spirit, of a devotional temperament delightfully suited to our company. I am truly abashed also, for she has a remarkable familiarity with the beast she calls "our Unicorn," and speaks readily of that strange and venerable creature as if he were her familiar pet and not the ancient guardian of mystic paths. In

Saturday, of May the Beginning

Last night I returned alone, weary of travel, and under the starlight gave most wholehearted thanks to God for this domain where we find such sweet refuge! My brief sojourn in Firenze left me in bafflement and disarray. But today I clearly see how that city's magnificent intellectual ferment is but the flush of a fever arising from a bottomless emptiness of faith.

Those noble men, many of them my friends and fellow students of old, all vie to surpass one another and profess mastery of things of which they dwell in utter ignorance. To think that the beauty of

their frail works can conquer death! And at the core of all their ceaseless activities lies a discontent so profound that it grieves my heart.

To none of them did I speak of the precious Unicorn, for their proud minds would have considered him either a fanciful myth or a scientific curiosity. Even so, I caused them great amusement, for to their eyes I have become a child again, a superstitious rustic clinging to dim fables in this age of changing ways and bold discovery. If these men are to shape the years to come, then my heart cries out, for those times will prove harsh and inhospitable to our modest, friendly creature and his subtle ways—driving him to retreat still further from the paths of Man.

But let others mold the world! Tomorrow, at last, I go into my retreat.

Sunday, of May the 2nd; at Dawn

Eugnostos has bidden that I take with me neither paper nor pen. I here confess that my past seclusions have been mostly dry and difficult, largely relieved by my books and writings. Yet I must now trust my Master.

Eugnostos says: "Only when thou drinkest from the rivers of silence wilt thou learn to sing."

Sunday, of May the 9th

Have I not heard the tale of the man who dug for turnips and found gold? My retreat is done!

For years I have tempered my mind with the divine art of alchemy, bathed in the mystical teachings of the Emerald Tablet, probed the secrets of Kabbalistic doctrine, sojourned with the anchorites of Scete. But now I have met the Unicorn face to face, and I am undone; for nothing had prepared me for the fiery touch of his wonderous mind.

Three days I passed in reverie and prayer, until at last I sat in sunlight by my open door, and I was content; and he came at last and laid his thoughts on mine. And I, willing and trusting, moved with them, filled with sweetness and strange images, seemingly from times so remote as to be beyond reckoning. Finally I could contain no more, and his touch began to burn too brightly. I was overcome, but the creature withdrew and vanished from my sight.

Now I understand the secret of that little hut, and why all our company displays such eagerness to retire there. For the Unicorn must dwell nearby—or could it be that a portal to his secret realm is not far hence?

After that first meeting I saw the Unicorn each day—but no more will I write, but this: here is an ancient mystery beyond compare. And yet the creature (can this be true?) is now my friend.

Says Eugnostos: "In friendship, there is no other goal but the uncovering of the spirit."

Tuesday, of May the 11th

After the noon meal, the blessed Eugnostos called me to his chamber. He asked me why I supposed there exist no true accounts of the Unicorn and answered himself, saying, "The Unicorn is not drawn to clerics and philosophers like ourselves, but rather to the youthful and innocent. Those few scholars fated to meet the magical beast were marvelously emptied of their burdensome learning and were ever after disinclined to write or speak of their encounters—for the memory of the Unicorn is like a shining taper that words would only dim."

Then Eugnostos smiled as if amused, saying, "But I see some special destiny has singled out thee to do this work."

"What work?" I asked, not comprehending.

"Doth not thy hand still crave to write and draw? Then write and draw thou must, and record the truth and history of the Unicorn. It seems that a divine purpose is here to be revealed, and thy skill may bear great fruit in the end. Work diligently, and let us look to a swift conclusion of the whole labor. But be not indiscreet, and keep the work secret. Hast thou not seen the sad fate of thy several friends, so dazzled by their own gifts that, unknowing, they have lost their way?"

Then our Master discharged me of all my other duties and bade me go and write. Thus humbled, but exhilarated, I departed his chamber.

Wednesday, of May the 12th

Plainly the proper shape for this undertaking must be a book, large and grand. On the order of this book:

—It must begin with the primeval conception of the Unicorn, describing as accurately as possible the forces that brought him into existence.

—And how he quickens life

—And of the Four Ages

—And of his attitudes and movements; of his duties, his divisions, and ranks; and of his visits with men. I shall ignore the many falsehoods and confusions abounding on this subject and present the simple truth. And this book's purpose shall be to instruct the earnest pilgrim on how he may encounter the Unicorn.

Let it begin with an illumination, in the manner of those found in rich breviaries, that the book may find favor in the eyes of God and men.

On the History and Truth of the Unicorn ❧

In Thee is concealed a strange and terrible mystery.

I, MAGNALUCIUS, BORN IN THE VILLAGE OF ANCHIANA in the year 1457, do set forth this work in my own hand and attest to its veracity. By God's grace, I have not lacked education, having first been trained in the art of drawing. But in its inks and pigments I found only pride and emptiness. So then I turned to books of natural philosophy and alchemy, even to the sacred Kabbala of the Hebrews. The most profound teachings of the Gnostic brethren I pursued in the cities and monasteries of Egypt. And in all these studies I learned hidden secrets, many and great.

Yet all I learned in those years was as a shadow in the light of the Unicorn, whose coming set the keystone to all my knowledge. All before had been first fruits, now harvest abounding.

Now this work pays no heed to the vain fancies and foolish imaginings of anyone, though they may have acquired the weight of hallowed tradition. As says Saint Columban, flower of the cloisters of Ireland: "Manifestly ancient is error, but the truly ancient is truth." If common lore long asserted by the wise and accepted by the majority is here contradicted, let the reader be satisfied that these words and pictures are witness to pure and simple experience, and judge the truth for himself.

O Reader: If thou art neither scribe nor sacrificer, cast not thy gaze upon this book, for it contains secret teachings useful only to the few and troubling to the many. And if thou seekest only mere amusement, read no further. But if thou art an earnest pilgrim on the path of Life, then open, read, and ponder.

The Book of Generation ❧

and breathed into it intelligence, so that it might become a spirit of harmony and guidance unto every corner of the void. This was the powerful spirit called Galgallim, whirling itself through uncounted ages while ever spiraling around the central Light. And while some things still fell into darkness, yet Galgallim guided others on a more rarified path toward the shores of Light. In such a way was balance achieved once more.

Then the Holy One wished for a panel on which to display His greater art; and between the shores of Light and the walls of darkness He hung in balance the Earth. Its naked mountains He raised in fire and scattered them with shining gems that still reflect those flames. Then the Holy One addressed the spirit of guidance, which is Galgallim, saying, "Out of the hidden gulfs I made thee, free and by form unbounded. Wilt thou accept shape upon Earth, that thou mayst supply a service even greater?"

And even as it was asked, so it was agreed.

The Book of Generation ❧

Mind on mind in wordless thought, these things the Unicorn made known to me:

The creature's true origins lie in the depths of Time, in that beginningless Beginning when all was emptiness and waste, darkness and mist. Then moved the Holy One to sunder the dark from the bright. So were established concord and balance, with darkness driven to the fringes and the Abode of Light at the middle point of all.

But darkness, once given a situation and compass for itself, grew weighty beyond accounting, intruding among all things and drawing them toward itself according to their weights and inclinations.

Therefore was the balance made to tremble, and from that trembling arose a resonance—an awesome sound that circled in the vast emptiness, chanting mightily. The Holy One modulated that sound to make of it a chord of great sweetness,

IN THE LONG, BRIGHT YEARS OF THE FIRST AGE, Man and Unicorn dwelt together, and both races grew in stature of body and mind. But other beings had been spawned in darkness, and in darkness grew strong.

De Libro Nemeseos

De Draconis Generatione

Ignis et Aqua

Draco primus vocabatur Yaldabaoth [quiet vocatur Tiamat, et illigatur multa alia nomina praeterea]

The Spawning of the Dragons

On that very day when the Unicorn drew forth from barren rock a gushing spring of life, the seeds of doom were sown as well. For even as those shining waters spread their fertile moisture, they poured into unlighted fissures and trickled down to secret, burning caverns that wound among the mountains' roots.

There, in those abysmal chambers, the sacred waters' life-bestowing charge was first expended in raising up a living thing. And thus in fire and in darkness was the Dragon born. Her nature bears everlasting testimony to that uneasy birth, and ever after, no other creature has possessed the same measure of strength and cunning.

Now the first dragon was Yaldabaoth (though she is called Tliamat as well, and many other names besides). She was fearsomely wrought, with darting, lidless eyes; and the first sight caught in her unblinking gaze was her own image, reflected in the dark waters. She worshipped the sight, and a secret lust for that selfsame image has consumed her heart for all time since.

And Yaldabaoth grew great and spawned others like herself: Nagamat and Kaliyat and Orkus, Tarasque and Serpens; and many more besides. Now while dragons are of many sizes and shapes, all are swift and sharp of intellect, and thirst after knowledge. While the Unicorn seeks to divine the secrets of creation that he may more perfectly know the Creator, the Dragon desires the same that it may gain dominion over all the world, and thereby conquer death.

Now the Dragon fiercely hates the Unicorn for his primacy, because it is not self-created, but owes to him its being. And so it has ever been the bane of the Unicorn, its fixed intent being to devour him, that it may no longer be an aftercomer, but be Oldest of All Things.

Now the Unicorn oversees all dominions of this world, and so in shadows and in fading light he finally

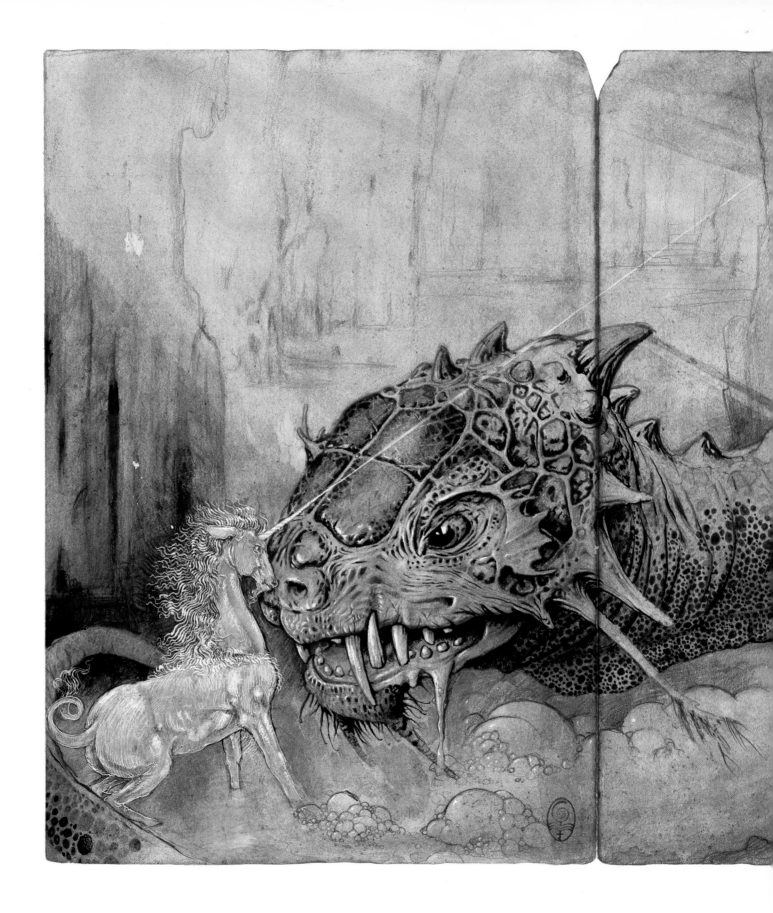

must confront the Worm. No creature exceeds the Unicorn in quickness or in courage, but vast and subtle is the knowledge of the Dragon. It can mold its mind to his and lure him into the mazes of its thought, where the Unicorn

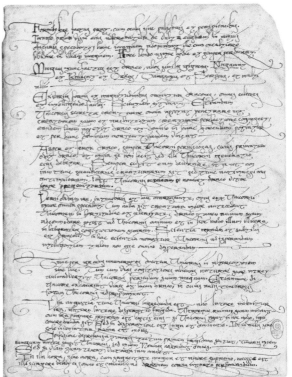

tarries, judging that such intelligence cannot be utterly without redemption. And so, by imperceptible degrees is he lead into a debate unending; while the Dragon drains him of his strength and light. In those sunless halls his doom approaches; and only when he treads paths of thought that utterly violate his nature does he realize how grim his plight has become.

Then must the Unicorn traverse a narrow path. On the one side waits hatred; on the other, cold despair. Either will prove his defeat; for to succumb to hate would be to grasp his enemy's own device and perish in its fire. Yet if he flees, despairing and depleted, then will he be overtaken, be undone, and perish.

Meshed in confusion, the Unicorn knows for the first time the cold touch of the fear suffered by mortal men; the only fear that he shall ever know. But if he be steadfast, victory may still be claimed. With great sagacity, with highest love, he must awaken as from a dream and, without hesitation, pierce the Dragon with his Spiral Horn.

25

On the Garden of the Unicorn (which is the First Age, and how Man departed thence) ❧

Ferebat profundam innocentiaque gratiaque vtroque genera. Touebant in saeculi aurei meridiem.
Ntendum tempora numerabant, que ineffabili gaudio vrgebantur.

On the Limits of the Garden

Now the Garden shone with a holy light, as on a joyous morning when the dew still sparkles and every leaf is green. Broad was its span upon the fields of earth, but beyond it lay ice-capped mountains where fires burned within, and wild places where the whirlwind roared and voices made themselves heard in the shining abyss.

The Unicorn can thrive in the midst of thunder and tempest and earthquake, but these awful heights were unsafe for Man. So as an elder, friend, and guide, the Unicorn trod the Garden's borders to watch lest any men venture outside its lawful limits.

Days then had little meaning, and time passed in unaccounted bliss. Even now the memory lingers of that unsullied glory, which is why even our sweetest quietude is touched with a sense of exiled longing. For Man multiplied in numbers and grew strong, and the Unicorn likewise; and together in full grace and innocence of mind these kindred races entered the noontide of the Golden Age. Then were forged those bonds that all time shall not break asunder, so that however lengthy our parting, Man and the Unicorn shall never meet as strangers.

The Coming of Serpens the Deceiver

[On verso of same sheet, not shown:]

But Yaldabaoth and her offspring brooded in vast vaults beneath the earth, and ever grew more jealous until at last they sent forth Serpens, the most cunning of their number. In size, it was minor and so struck no fear in the hearts of men. Rather they thought the Dragon comely and wondrous, for its scales were fiery and of all hues, and its words were finely chosen; and soon it was moving among Man as one familiar, clouding its purpose, as is the Dragon's craft. That is, it interwove words of praise with ones of doubt, saying, "What a wise and worthy ruler

Man might have been!" and its every discourse lamented that the Unicorn should restrain his friends within the Garden.

Not all our race heeded these subtle lures of pride and discontent. Even from the first days, male and female were allotted their different intuitions; and so women were not deluded by Serpens' guile, but retained trust in their hearts, loving the Unicorn no less. But when at last Serpens heard men grumble that the Unicorn might be a less than perfect friend and bent instead on selfish wiles, then it spoke more openly. Beyond the Garden, the Dragon claimed, lay lands both fair and ripe for Man's dominion—a legacy denied him by the Unicorn, who held Man captive lest he grow too numerous to govern.

Now these lies did not escape the notice of the Unicorn, who walked in sorrow, and alone. For he could not compel Man to the paths of light, but only point the way; and in the debates of their untempered wisdom, no men sought his counsel. And of these, the most deluded rose up, crying, "Let us break our golden chains and bid farewell to bondage! And if the longer, harder path we choose, far brighter shall the ending be!"

Thereafter, for all the ills and sorrows that would befall, men could not blame any but themselves. For the rest cried out in loud approval, even as the women bowed their heads in silent grief. And thus the Dragon's work was done, and so these words became the doom of Man.

27

On the Changing of the Age

Then Moved the Holy One, in perfect accord with Man's ill-conceived intents. And within the hour, the springtime world grew hard and dim. And it seemed that forgetful emptiness descended on men's minds, and when that darkness was lifted up, behold, they found themselves in a denser realm, a shadow of their former one. Uncertainly at first they moved, being clad in coarser form. And from that hour was counted the beginnings of the Second Age, called the Age of Silver.

The Sundering of the Kindred Races

Now it is not within my compass to chronicle each age, nor the bitter path that led Man to this fourth and final world. Only this needs be said: that Man fell into a moral slumber, worshipping idols and fighting against his neighbor. And through all these afteryears, Man and Unicorn grew ever more apart, as Yaldabaoth and her kind had wished.

Then did the Unicorn go upon his separate way while Man stood firm in folly, and thus their mingling was at an end. But while the Garden of that golden realm remains his rightful home, the creature's heart is still bound to Man, and so ever he travels across the sundry worlds to linger at our present boundaries.

And even now may a man meet the Guide, if he but waken from that fretful sleep [of error].

The Seven Houses ❧

TRULY, THE UNICORN DISPLAYS A GREAT VARIETY OF shapes, sizes, and temperaments, from the delicate deer-like Avarim to the bold Arweharis that guards the night.

Now all unicorns belong to one of seven Houses, which have their sundry duties and domains.

This is a difficult study, for I have seen a unicorn confronted by danger seem to grow more robust in size and musculature. There may be no final shape to which the beast must hold.

Eugnostos says, "Observe the Unicorn. Consider his beauty. Close thine eyes; then look again. That which thou seest was not before—and that which was, is no longer."

By Asallam, the Penetrating, the Mighty, the Firstborn, were the life-giving waters brought forth. And in his Garden, Asallam begat Ilvilon the Devoted, called the Friend of Man; then Vata, who shall come at the dawn of the End of Days. And Ohani, and Kestevara, and Abram, and Isfendarmad, who knows the darkness.

From these, the Seven Protectors, are descended every unicorn in the Seven Houses.

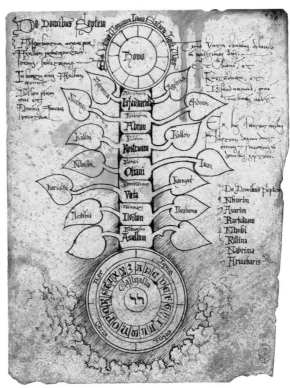

29

Avarim

Inter domos septem, Avarim praecipue hominibus nocituri suut valde
numerosae in regno nostro sunt et in rebus nostris valde intermiscuntur.
Regnis Occidentalis dispensatores   Qui enim non gustavit de praesentia
sunt illae, portitores officiorum   dulci Avarim
multorum et laboriosarum. Ad nos   Gaudium certum sed caducum, desiderium cordis
mortales invisibiliter accedunt per   exaltatio spiritus, halitus tremor quasi
fines generum nostrum furtim   dolens. Temporis punctum evanescens, nac
currentes   statim oblitus aut vercibus quae sommis
                                        deditus

The Unicorn in His Battle Rapture ❧

THE GREATER BEASTS OF PREY share a blind and arrogant savagery, and sometimes they will assault the Unicorn. He will never flee, for this mystical beast is not lawful prey, and no animals should remain so deluded. Then is his most peaceful demeanor transformed into mortal fury, and his unexcelled attack swiftly dismays even the boldest creatures of this world. Nor will the Unicorn relent in his fearsome wrath until his adversaries repent or are slain.

In battle, he falls upon his foes like a bright spear of flame. His merciless pointed hooves are quick and accurate. But his Horn is an instrument of healing and of knowledge, and never will he employ it in mortal combat, lest it be fouled with blood.

The Tempest 🦋

THE UNICORN EXULTS IN THE TEMPEST and braves the fiercest blasts, rarely seeking shelter, for these raw displays of nature's power are to him a pale reminder of the swirling forces of his birth.

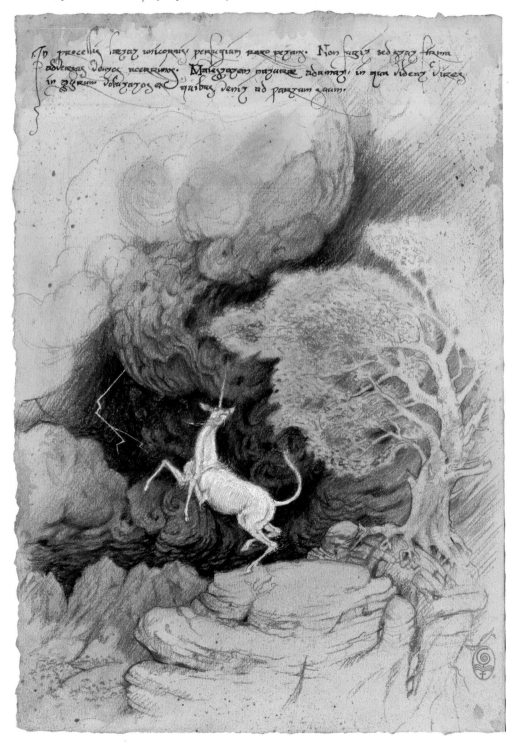

Of the Unicorn's Conduct with Other Creatures ❦

ALL ANIMALS LOVE HIM, FOR *among the beasts he is the most affectionate. Even with his superior intelligence and transcendent nature, yet he is still an elder brother of their kind; and his mere presence quickens in them a dim awareness of their own highest nature and divine creation.*

. . . [Each] animal employs some rudimentary language of sound or movement, and the Unicorn seems quickly to master whatever signals he may encounter.

41

THE UNICORN REJOICES IN the languages of Man, listening to them from afar. But in them he finds no matters useful for contemplation, for words to him are but trivial exercises by which Man shows off his clever mental plumage.

In truth, the mind of the Unicorn is unlike ours. Keen are his perceptions and his intelligence, but he has no power of deep abstraction. Speculation and contentious arguing too are absent from his nature. Instead, his thoughts are drawn from natural things, revealed in their entirety by his pure vision. Many contraries naturally resolve themselves in his instinctive mind in endlessly repeating patterns and variations, as a musical harmony among otherwise dissonant tones.

But though Man and Unicorn are so unlike in their inclinations, yet we may still converse with him—for how else could I bring forth these lofty mysteries?

I have learned how easily the Unicorn can rest his mind upon a man's or maiden's thoughts and distinguish the secrets cloistered there! And in the keenness of these moments, some mortals become sensible to the subtle movements of Unicorn thought and, surrendering by degrees to its gentle currents, are led to gaze into the sanctuary of his inner mind.

O MAN, REGARD THE UNICORN
with awe!

When thou gazest into his eyes, gird thyself; for he knows all the history of our Race, and his unbroken memories reach back across the darkness of the years to vast and powerful dominions, now utterly undone by Fate and Time.

Know that the Earth has changed her face: lands have slipped beneath the waves of the sea. Rivers have not been faithful to their courses, nor mountains steadfast in their shapes. If thou wouldst know those things that went before, seek thou the Spiral Horn.

He points the way,
He guards the gate,
He waits until the End.

On Maidens ❦

BETWEEN THE UNICORN AND MAIDENS LIES A SECRET BOND not known by men.

For men marvel at the Unicorn, the sight filling them with reverence, or fear, or even mystical desire. But in women, the Unicorn evokes only that simple tenderness peculiar to their gender, to which the Unicorn is drawn like a bee to a fragrant flower.

And in this attraction lies a sweet mystery! For by degrees, the Unicorn forsakes his lonely privacy, becoming—if I may say so—the maiden's pet, or as an innocent child who trustingly surrenders to the soft caresses of a mother's care.

The Maid, for her part, is made sensible of that divine power that nurtures all living things, and comes to know it is a power hardly lacking in her being.

To any woman may this sweet friendship be granted, for age and station are of no account, only that she possess chastity of heart. For the creature requires not that she has never known the touch of men, only that an untempered longing for that touch has not closed her inner vision, nor goaded her into a hungry desire for the pleasures of the world! For the Unicorn dwells at the very margins of our realm, and those entangled in visible delights can never follow him, but only those with an open and trusting heart.

And women have not the thirst for domination over others by which men are constantly possessed. Those who crave dominion seldom suffer themselves to be led, so how can they wisely select a guide to point their way?

Know yourselves, brethren: Are ye as wise as ye flatter yourselves to be? He who wishes to lead, let him learn to follow!

[On reverse of same sheet, not shown:]

Eugnostos informs me that I have not got parts of this quite correct:—That the maiden and the Unicorn are more like chaste and secret lovers.—And that a virgin ignorant of corporeal desire is more likely to receive wisdoms of the spirit.

On the Unicorn's Friendship with an Ancient Race ❦

[Continued from a previous page, not shown:]

I CONSIDERED THE WILD MEN MERELY A TALE TO FRIGHTEN children. Yet now the Unicorn has shown me this strange and curious people.

The Old Ones, as so they term themselves, are indeed a hoary stock whose songs recall the Age before the Flood; they are the Unicorn's favorite consorts. Long before the founding of Rome they ranged all over these lands, and named the stars, and raised their standing stones. But now they are few, and faded into the trackless woods.

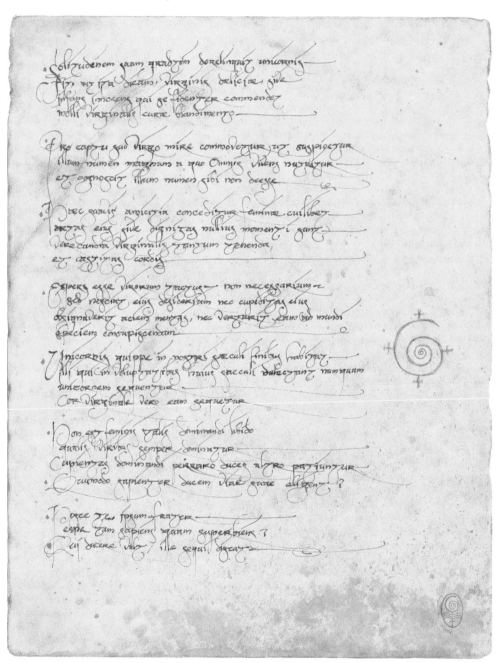

In appearance they are wild indeed, clothing themselves in animal skins and pounded bark adorned with amulets of polished stone and bronze, wearing their hair free and uncut. But closer observation reveals their quiet, gentle nature and subtle ways.

Among them the Unicorn walks easily and unconcerned, and they receive him as a relative or trusted friend, with little ceremony. He has taught them the healing herbs, the portents in the flight of birds, the language of trees, and many other secret lore besides.

Their gods forbid them to touch iron, or use the wheel, or eat the flesh of swine, or kill any living thing without a prayer. Their woodcraft is unexcelled. They pass through the trees silently as the owl, but in their leafy forest home, they can no longer view the stars.

Ever their numbers diminish, for each spring their forest borders are hewn and plowed, and now is the twilight of their years. To their fate the Old Ones seem quietly resigned. They say that the Earth is drawing them, like a fallen oak moldering on the forest floor, back into her dark and peaceful womb; but that someday they will come again, and raise their stones anew to count the stars.

Of the One Who Is Beyond Laws ❧

NOW A MAN FREELY BELIEVES HIMSELF a man, and will declare himself a drover or merchant, prince or monk according to his station in life. But no leaping stag did ever halt himself to think, "I am a stag;" and neither does the Unicorn. For his free mind

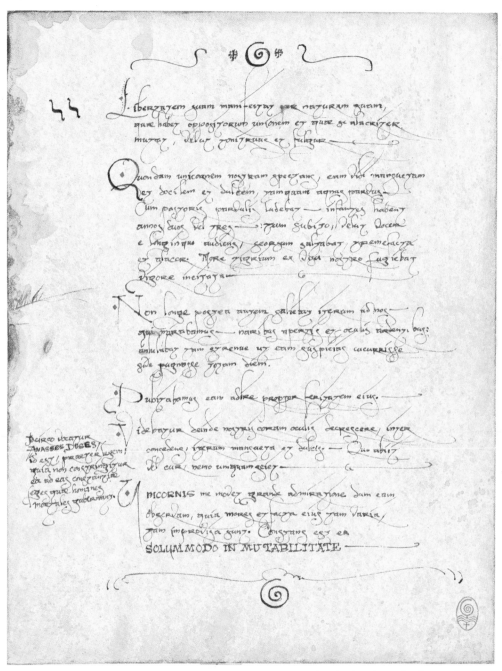

Once I gazed upon our Unicorn and saw him to be gentle and docile, sweet as a young lamb. He was playing on the grass with a shepherd's children, but two or three years of age. Then suddenly, as if hearing a call from a great distance, he leapt to one side, all trembling and alert. And in the manner of a tiger pursued by dreadful forces, he fled from our sight.

Where he went and why, no one shall ever know. But not many minutes had passed when, to our surprise, he came bounding back, nostrils flaring and eyes ablaze and panting so vigorously that one would have thought he had run all day. And so fierce and savage was his mien that we hesitated to draw too near to him.

Then before our eyes he seemed to diminish, and again knelt among the little ones, once more tame and gentle.

The Unicorn stirs me with great wonderment the more that I regard him, so diverse and unpredictable are his deeds and habits. In truth, he is constant only in his mutability. Wherefore, he is called Anasses Duses; that is, the Lawless One, who is not constrained by the consistencies that govern mortal Man.

does not cast its thoughts in those deadly molds of habit and happenstance. Instead, he knows himself to be a spirit, who tarries as a Unicorn.

This freedom he makes known by his perplexing nature, which contains a union of opposites and abruptly alters itself, like thunder and lightning.

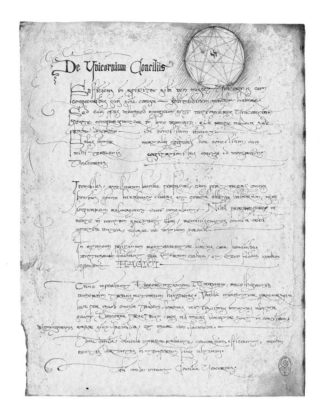

In his spirit, the Unicorn is sufficient unto himself and does not mingle with his own kind without reason, preferring the dignity of solitude. But when some great need comes to pass, the more ancient of the unicorns gather, unbidden and of their own accord, in some remote place, whether lofty crag or secret glade. And there they hold their council.

While through all the lands men relax their cares in sleep, the unicorns stand motionless, drenched in the light of the stars. Abandoning the use of tongues, not at all in haste, from mind to mind they gaze, thinking back over all the ages gone by, even to the very roots of Time when the Earth was new. And there, restored to that primeval state, the unicorns make new their ancient covenant with Man, and to the Holy One pledge again their faith.

Then they begin the Great Recollection, and call forth the long histories of ages past; and the council marvels how all things have at last assumed those forms prefigured at their birth. And finally do they come upon the questions of the present hour, distinguishing the needs that must be fulfilled from those better left undone.

At the last, even as dawn is reddening the hills, the unicorns make their harmony complete; and as one, they turn their minds outward to the End of Time.

So was I taught, for the Unicorn stripped me of inferior thought and showed me, alone among men, the way in which the unicorns hold council.

52

decision. Now, the left seemed to breathe an air of mystery and dark secrets. I boldly advanced my steps that way, and the Unicorn followed.

Before long, the trees became fantastical and wildly gnarled. Below them loomed strange rocky outcrops that inflamed my imagination until, in truth, I fancied that I had joined the ranks of ancient heroes. Through me coursed an unfamiliar vitality. My every sinew thrilled with the thought of great and awesome deeds, and like a fearsome warrior, I strode forward to meet my Destiny.

Dark and moist was the air. Winding through a misty swamp, the path contracted itself to a ribbon of smooth black stones. Then all at once both fen and forest gave way, and before me rose a tall cliff. Into it was cut a fissure both narrow and dark, the surrounding rock peculiarly weathered, as if ancient runes had been etched there. As I stared deep into the mountain's heart, a soft voice from within the defile spoke, saying, "Magnalucius!" It was like a whisper, intimate and near, yet cold as stone; and it seemed learned and most reasonable, speaking words of great interest to me, and welcoming me forward.

I was sorely inclined to obey. Yet my legs refused to move and fell to trembling so that I could scarcely stand. Then the Unicorn touched me gently from behind. I turned and

fled from that grim abode, looking back but once. And in that stony defile I beheld two fearsome eyes, set in a scaly head.

When we came again to that massive, worthy oak, I paused and was moved to ponder that I had nearly stumbled into a dragon's snare. But seeing that the Unicorn had started down the right-hand path, I cast aside my musings and hastened after him.

Now this path was green with soft moss and strewn with tiny flowers. Upon it, my tread seemed coarse and clumsy, so I removed my dusty sandals and left them beside the way. We soon entered a stand of tall, graceful trees of a species unknown to me. Smooth and slim were their twigs, with lacy foliage of silver-green. My heart was lightened by the music of running waters and the sweet calls of many birds. Then security and great peace descended upon me, for I saw that my Fate would come; I did not need to seek it out, and needed only follow that bold and shining Horn, and not trouble myself where it should lead.

How long we walked that lovely, shaded pathway I know not, for though my heart was full, our passage was without incident, and time passed as if in a dream. At last the forest ended, and we stood atop a high precipice. Far below us spread a comely land adorned with springtime's splendor, and upon it

the sun shone so gloriously bright that every detail was perfectly
manifest, the furthest objects no less clear and distinct than those
nearby.

The view was wide and vast, yet at the same time
everything appeared small and precious, as if I could embrace
them all. My heart overflowed
with silent bliss at these wonders,
of which not the least was this:
The landscape I gazed on seemed
to be myself. And my eyes were
filled with tears, as one who comes
home at last from long and wintry
wanderings.

I was eager to seek a safe
path down that perilous cliff. But
it was not given me to linger there,
for the Unicorn led me back the
way we had come. Reluctantly I
trod behind him until the trees
became familiar and we emerged
from that small copse upon the
twin hills. And behold! the sun
had still not risen above the
eastern rim of the world.

The Unicorn lightly
bounded back into the trees, but I
knew that no ordinary search
would find him there. In joy and
sadness I sat in the growing light,
entertaining many thoughts and
speculations. But having glimpsed
that wondrous realm beyond the
Forest of Brocileande, nevermore
shall I find satisfaction in this
world we know.

[On reverse of same sheet, not shown:]

All that exists here is to be
found there also. But there, every
object seems to be the true original of
its kind, and newly created, of which
the examples we know are but pale
reflections. What pen can trace a
world without corruption? Or what
brush paint colors no eyes have seen
before?

Of the Secret Fraternity 🦄

MY UNDERSTANDING OF THE Unicorn deepened, and into my heart entered many things that had before escaped my notice. And this is one: that amongst us walk many men and women who secretly delight in the companionship of the Holy Beast.

Often they are wanderers or people of simple station. Dreamy-eyed, always considerate, but somewhat shy, they care but little for the things of this world.

Such a one, I learned to my surprise, is Taddeo, who regularly appears at our gate. I had always held this traveling tinker to be jolly, if somewhat irreverent, but an ordinary tradesman. Yet now I know otherwise: wherever his footsteps lead him, a certain unicorn is never far. The two are bound to one another in some way I cannot fathom.

IN THE HORN IS ALL OF THE UNICORN'S COMPLETE HISTORY.

In form it is a spiral: two halves or flutes being wound about each other. In his youth—or so the Unicorn measures time—his Horn displays a smooth and simplified appearance. The flutes are tightly wound, not unlike the strands that comprise a rope, and evidence a certain vibrant and compacted energy.

As the Unicorn progresses through his life, his Horn undergoes a remarkable transformation, the spiral elongating into a subtler twist. Now this well illustrates the Horn's living nature. In the fullness of his years, the gyre of this creature's Horn is even more relaxed. And further, with great age, the Horn acquires grooves and creases, which are the graven records of the lessons he has experienced.

The Unicorn appears to consider his Horn as a vessel, or a canal for his thoughts; or perhaps as the organ of an unnamed sense.

The Unicorn's term upon the earth is far greater than Man's. Yet he is subject, like all created things, to Time, and age, and final dissolution.

Now what is fair in Man is subject to decay: and every passing year will leave its imprint until, at the last, the mortal body crumbles into dust. Not so with the Unicorn, for even countless years do not mar his beauty; his twilight is as comely as his dawn. But when at last he dies, he perishes utterly and at once, never again to be seen in any realm until the end of Time. But his departure is not without its monument, for behind he leaves his Horn—adamantine, and charged with a deathless virtue.

In this way only may a horn be obtained, for neither force of arms nor web of sorcery can wrest this spiraled boon from its living owner.

Now of all the aspects of the Unicorn, what holds chief sway over the mind of Man is his Horn— spiraling, solitary, great, and powerful. Deservedly so, for that shaft is his talisman and his token also. In it is distilled all his strength, wisdom, and subtle understanding. This Horn is outward and visible, but is also the mystical and ungraspable form of this creature.

Neither forward nor to the rear does the Horn incline, but springs directly forth from the creature's level brow, a little above his eyes.

In hue it is shining white, whiter than snow, smoother than ivory—yet vibrant with life, even more so than mortal flesh, and wedded to farthest-seeing senses. At once it occupies both this and other realms, and is thus able to penetrate all substances.

In times of danger or unwavering mental concentration, the Horn can display a certain glimmer or soft glow.

On the True Horn, and a Riddle ❧

Friday, of March the 3rd

After the morning meal, Eugnostos summoned me to his chamber. Thence I repaired, taking with me some candied ginger, which I knew he favors.

I found him reading. The morning sun fell on his aged shoulders, and he seemed nearly as transparent as the ancient parchments of the book. He thanked me for the ginger, saying, "Nay, it is for thee. I have no more taste for such sweetmeats.

"One year has passed," he continued, "since the Unicorn first showed himself to thee. And in that time, he has revealed to thee more than thy brethren here shall ever know. Yet hast thou ceased thy painterly labors and put aside thy pen?"

"I have not," I replied, abashed.

"So be it! Today I shall instruct thee in a matter that the creature keeps mostly to himself. Attend:

"Though many are the Unicorn's years, yet they have a limit, for whatever exists in Time

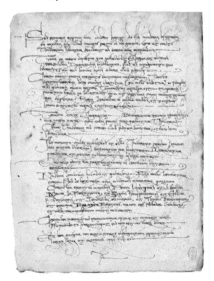

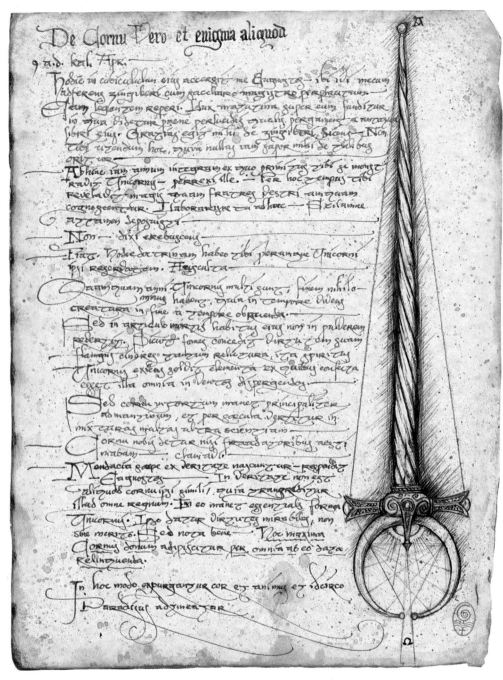

must be by Time undone. But when his death finally comes, his frame sinks not into decay. Just as tinder yields up its virtue to the flame and leaves but ash behind, so does the creature's departing spirit release all the elements in which it was divinely clothed; and straightaway they are scattered by the wind.

"But the Spiral Horn endures, for it is sovereign and adamantine and transmutes through the ages into many unknown compounds."

"Then the Horn is not merely an invention of swindlers and rogues?" I asked.

"Ofttimes, lies are born from truth!" replied Eugnostos. "And in truth, the Horn is like unto no other earthly thing, for it bridges every realm. In it, the essence of the Unicorn remains. To it are attributed marvelous powers—and not without reason. But mark: the Horn's greatest boon is gained by forsaking all that it can grant. In this manner both heart and mind may

be purified, and paradise attained. Yet greedy rumors have made the Horn an object of priceless value, such that many would gladly seek to slay the Unicorn and become its owner."

Then from his wooden chest, Eugnostos lifted something swaddled in damasked cloth and unwrapped it and held it in the sunlight. It was a mighty horn, set in archaic silver. Silently we gazed on it together, and the world seemed to open into a different kind of time. All haste was banished. The fleeting moment seemed to slow, encouraging the most lucid perception of every splendid detail. I heard Isabella's laughter in the kitchen and the soft scraping of a plow in the northern fields.

"Have you not wondered," asked Eugnostos at last, "why the Unicorn sojourns so frequently with our small fellowship? He is drawn by the virtue of the Horn—yea, even as we speak!"

At those words, I looked up to see a small unicorn (one I had not seen before) outside the window. It lingered but a moment, casting its gaze on our Master, and then stole away.

"How came this precious relic into thy possession?" I asked.

"There is no possession," he laughed, "unless the Horn possesses me. But of its history, a little I can tell thee. It has been with Bran Vendigard and Lleiver Mawr of Britain, with Zosimus of Panopolis and Gildas the Wise, and Iamblicus the Alchemist and Alcuin the Frank and Bayizad Bistami and Adelaide of Sicily, and many others of no worldly fame. The Horn passes to whom it chooses, and leaves again. Perhaps someday it may choose thee . . . but that is not for me to say."

Then Eugnostos fell silent. He would not explain this riddle, for he tires swiftly, and begged my leave to rest again.

The Prophecy
of the True Horn ❧

ACROSS THE VOIDS OF TIME DID THESE
words come to me.

◇

Into darkness will I fade,
Into a night that Man has made,
But through that gloom shall gleam the Sun
When I am lost, and again am won.

◇

Release! Release! I call to thee
In New Lands across the sea:
Let another, on narrow pathways, come to me.

◇

Furthest and Highest,
Yet not beyond reach.
Choose thou well a path that will teach
How the Sunken is raised
And Emptiness is filled
And a wandering heart
Can finally be stilled.

◇

Seek the Great Stone! Mark it well, with a sign,
That the one who shall follow
Shall see it is mine,
And, seeing, shall ponder and certainly know
As the Ancients have writ: "As Above, so Below."

◇

And I shall guard the Source of Greatness;
Waiting by a teardrop
From neither joy nor sorrow born,
In silver bound, beneath the ground,
I am the Spiral Horn.

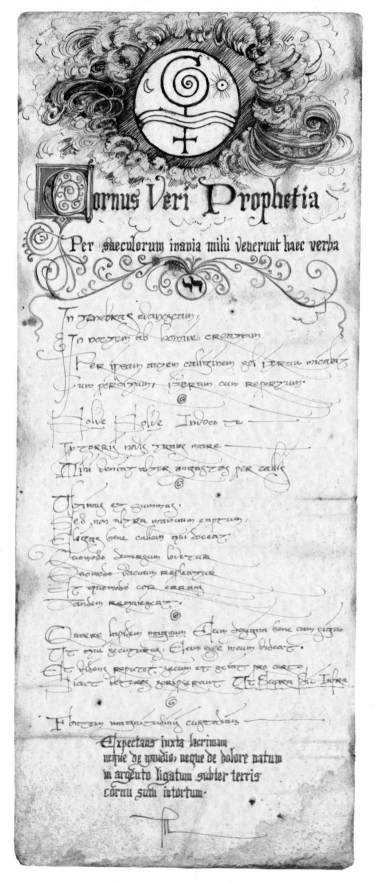